THE AMAZING VOYAGE OF JACKIE GRACE

by Matt Faulkner

SCHOLASTIC INC.
New York Toronto London Auckland Sydney

Created with love for Amy

ISBN 0-590-44860-9

12 11 10 9 8 7 6 5 4 3 2   5   1 2 3 4 5 6/9

Printed in the U.S.A.   08

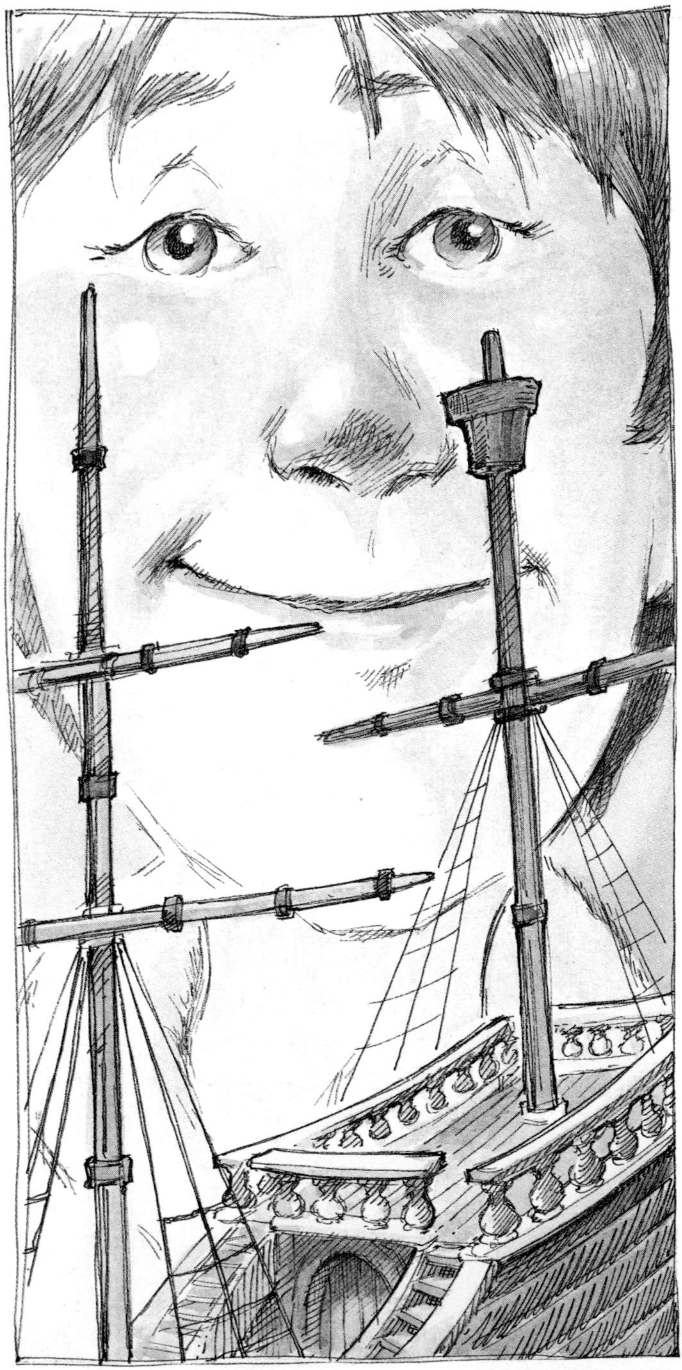

YO HO!
Yoho, I say, I'm coming aboard!

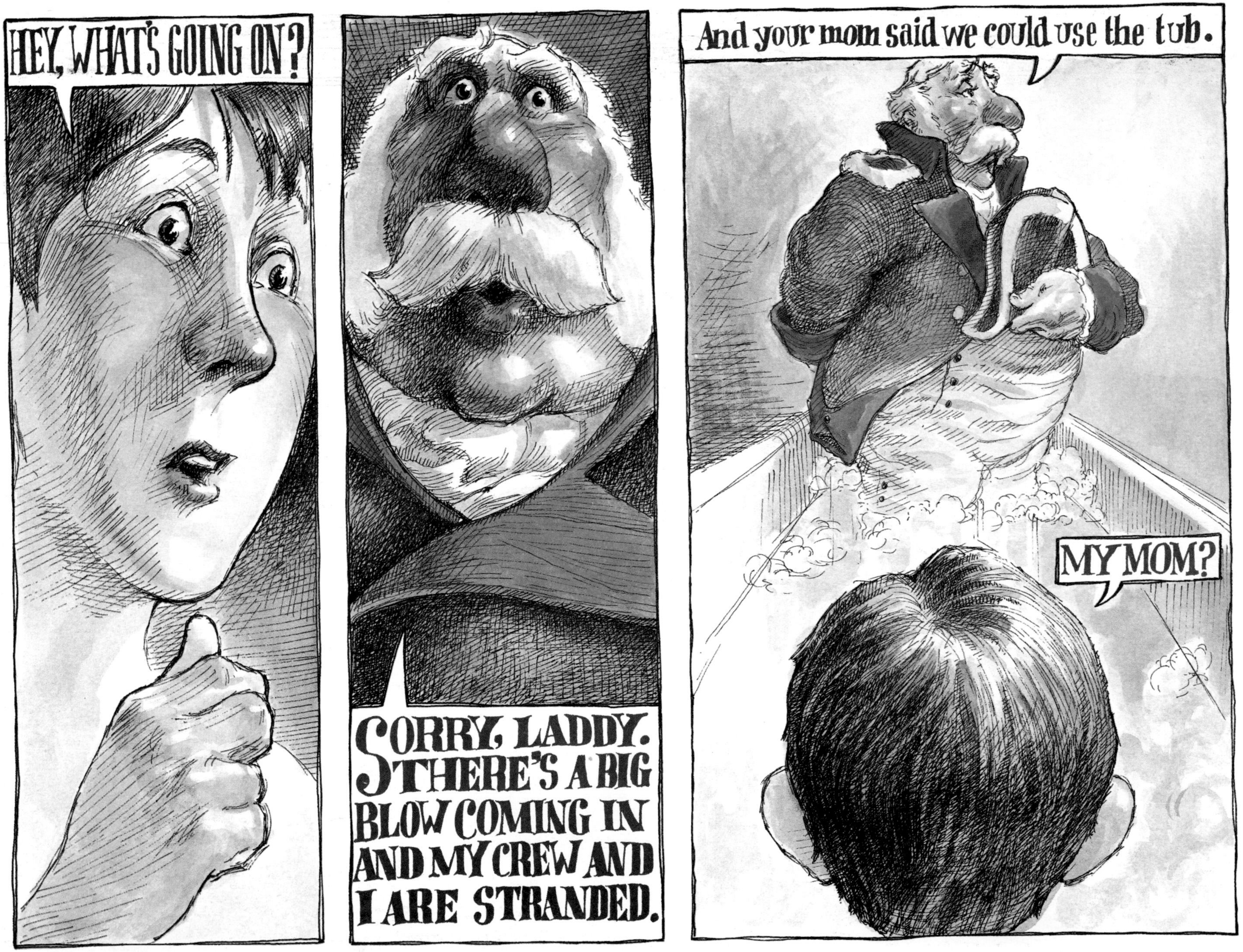
HEY, WHAT'S GOING ON?
SORRY, LADDY. THERE'S A BIG BLOW COMING IN AND MY CREW AND I ARE STRANDED.
And your mom said we could use the tub.
MY MOM?

Here's my crew now!

MOVE YOUR DUFFS, YOU LAZY OAFS!

And where have you two been?
It's his fault Cap'n, he...

STOP YOUR SQUEALING.
THAT TWISTER IS GOING TO ROLL OVER US ANY SECOND!
NOW WAIT A MINUTE.
OOOH · OW · OOO · OOOOH

THIS IS MY TUB AND I SAY...

THERE ISN'T ENOUGH ROOM FOR ALL OF US!
Better do somethin' with him, Cap'n. The storm's almost here!

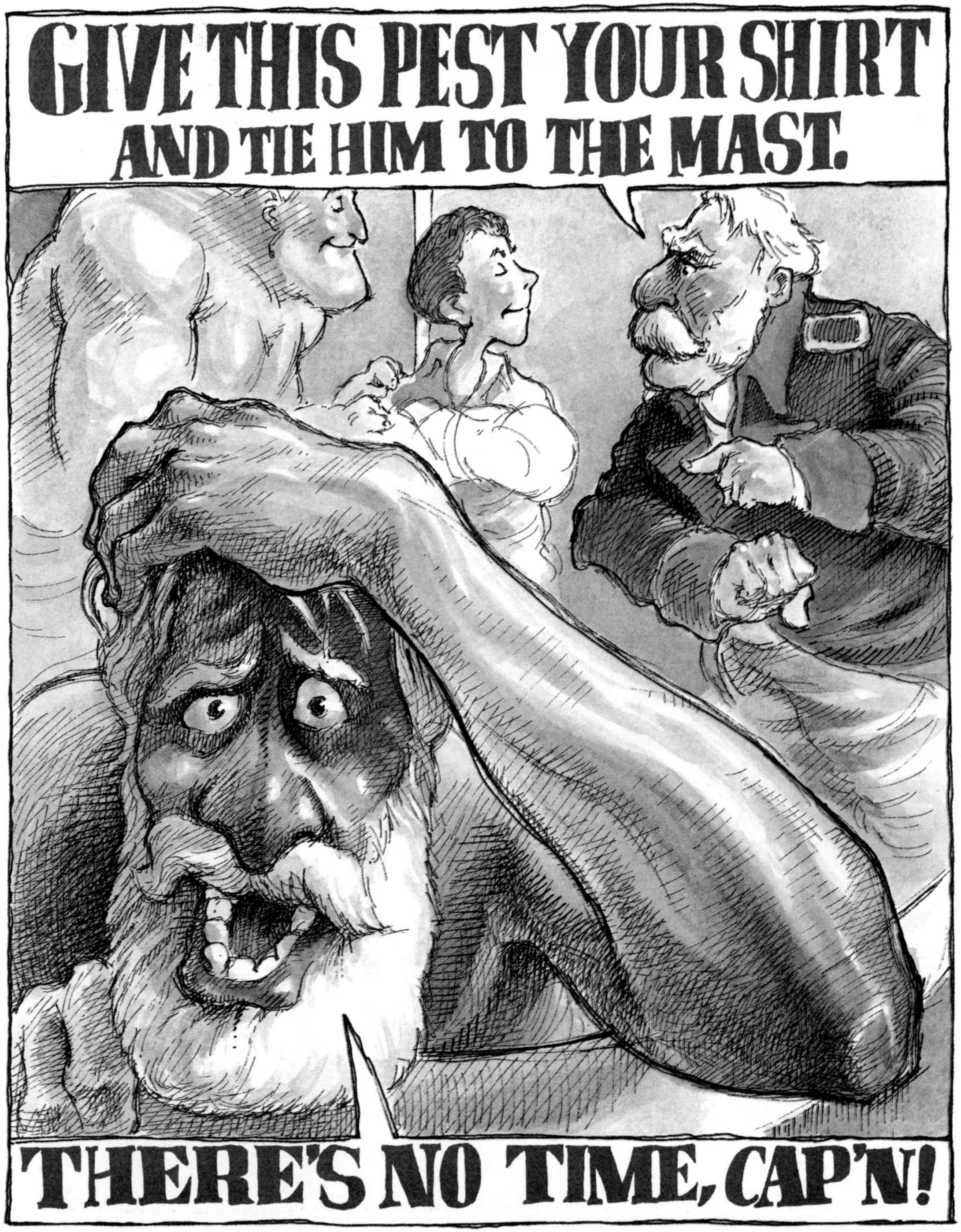
GIVE THIS PEST YOUR SHIRT AND TIE HIM TO THE MAST.
THERE'S NO TIME, CAP'N!

MOM
HERE IT COMES! PREPARE FOR ROUGH SEAS!

Wow.

ALL IS WELL!

RIG UP A SAIL!

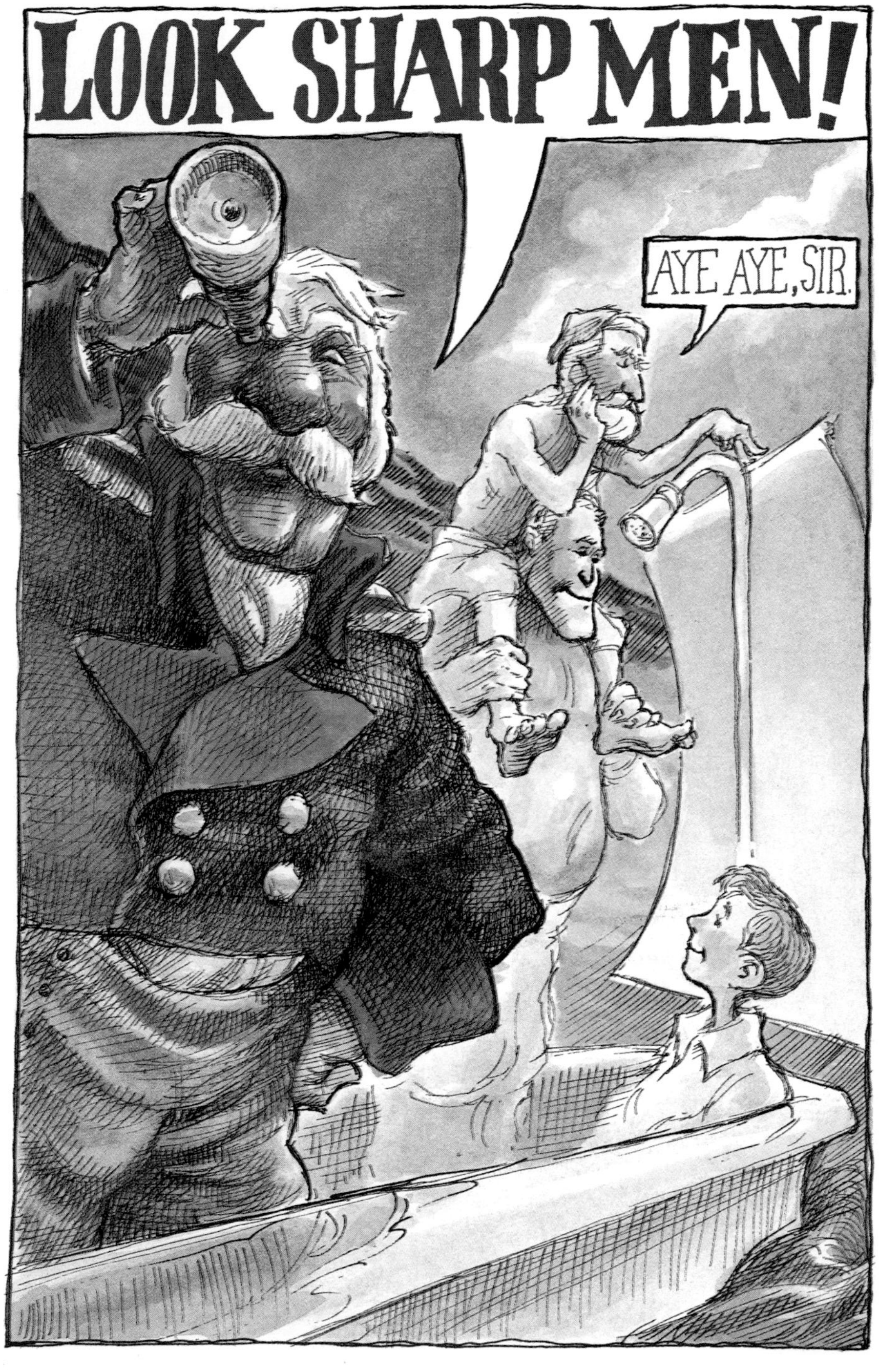
LOOK SHARP MEN!
AYE AYE, SIR.

SHIP AHOY!
THERE'S OUR SHIP, CAP'N.
THE CHASE IS ON!

IT WON'T BE LONG NOW, LADDY! WE'LL HAVE THOSE PIRATES RIGHT WHERE WE WANT THEM!
PIRATES?

OH BOY!

PREPARE TO ATTACK!

ATTACK?
STAY OUT OF THE WAY, BOY!

ATTENTION ALL PIRATES!
IF YOU LEAVE MY SHIP PEACEFULLY WE WON'T HARM YOU.

I shall count to THREE!
Fire when he gets to three!

ONE, TWO...
I CAN'T WATCH!

THREE!
FIRE!

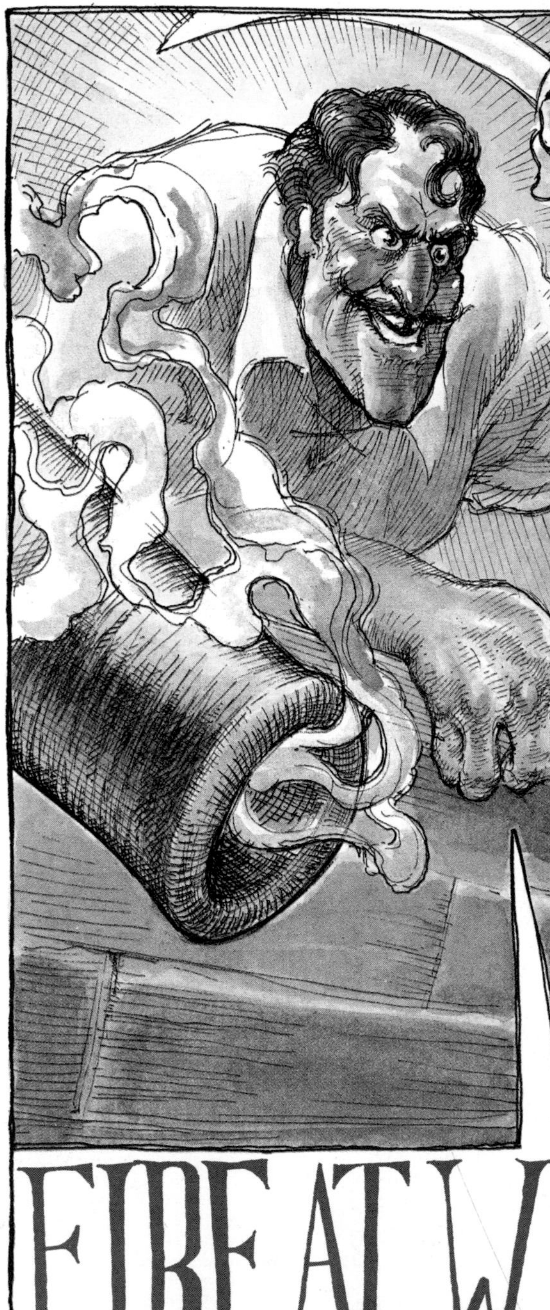
FIRE AT WILL!

WE'VE BEEN HIT!
WE'RE SINKIN', CAP'N!
OH DASH IT ALL.
NOW I'M GETTING MAD!

SORRY, OLD CHAP. IT LOOKS AS IF OUR LUCK HAS JUST RUN OUT.
WANNA BET?

NO LAD! STAY WITH THE SHIP!

WELL HELLO, RUNT.
WELCOME ABOARD! HA!

I'D SAY THIS LITTLE LAMB WAS LOST. WOULDN'T YOU, BOYS?
UH, YOUR BOOT IS UNTIED.

OH, THAT'S CUTE, MY BOOOOOOT!

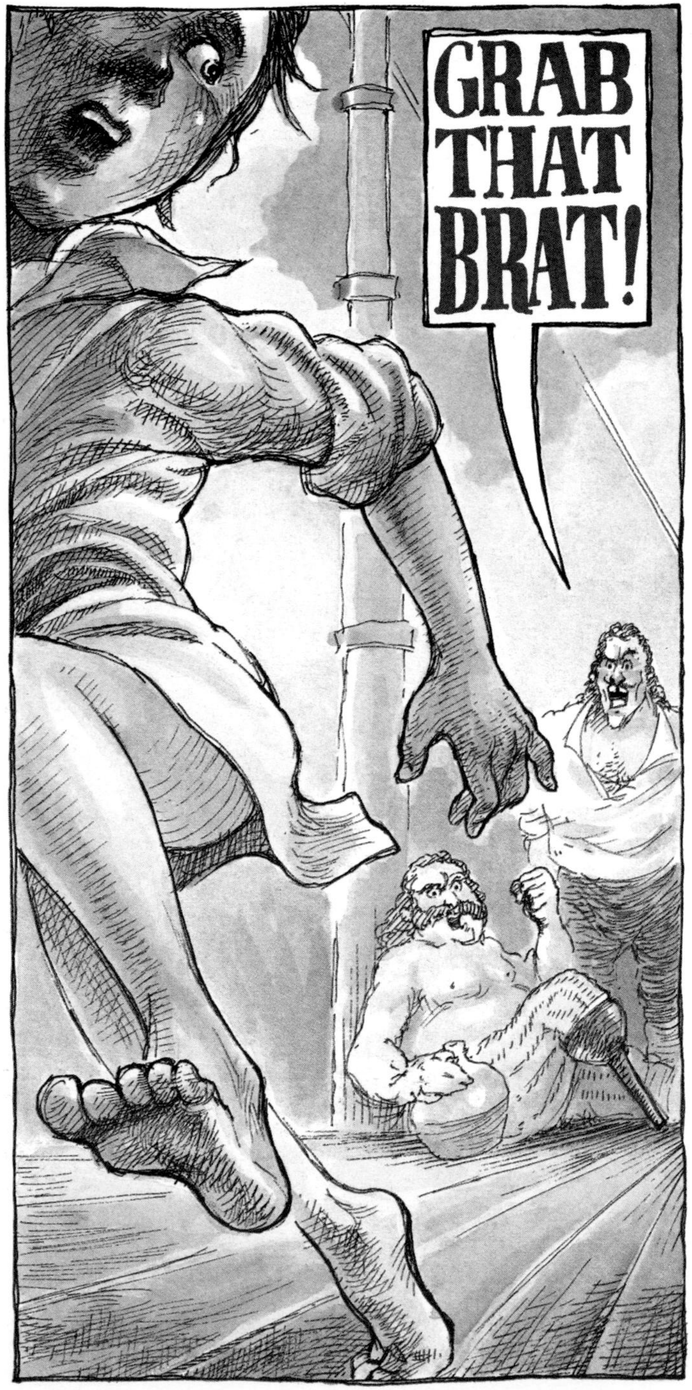
GRAB THAT BRAT!

Ooooop.

THUMP

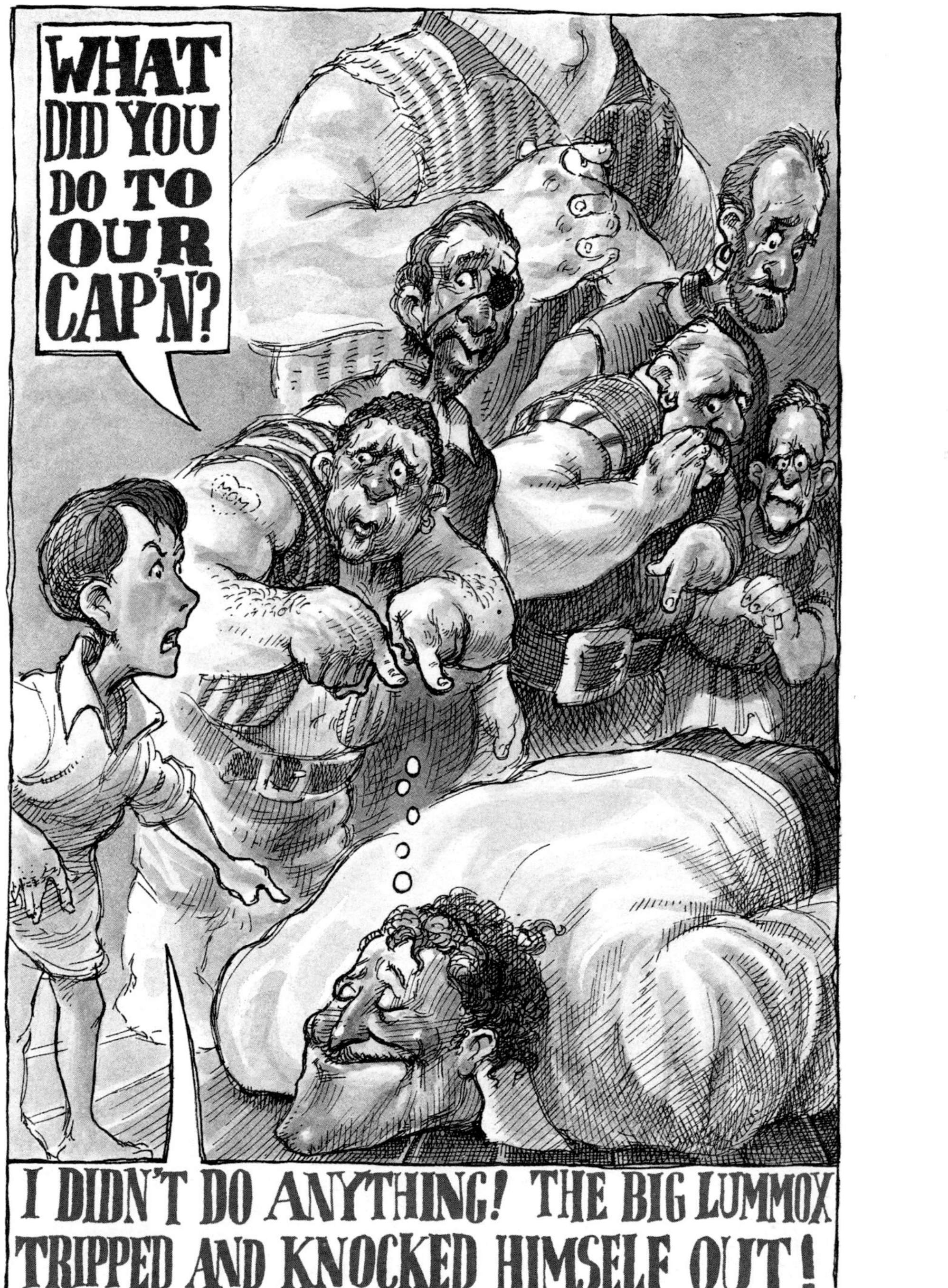
WHAT DID YOU DO TO OUR CAP'N?
MOM
I DIDN'T DO ANYTHING! THE BIG LUMMOX TRIPPED AND KNOCKED HIMSELF OUT!

RUN FER YER LIVES!
JUMP SHIP!
HEY! WHERE'S EVERYBODY GOING?

YIPES!
HE'S A MADMAN!
WHAT THE...
RUN AWAY!

WELCOME ABOARD, CAPTAIN!
OH, I SAY! GOOD SHOW!

YOU'RE A HERO, JACKIE!
WELL, NOT REALLY.

HEE HEE HEE!
WE'RE GONNA GIVE JACKIE THE REWARD FOR CAPTURIN' YOU!

JACKIE, I'D LIKE YOU TO JOIN MY CREW!
NO KIDDING?

COUNT ME IN, CAPTAIN!

I CAN HEAR THE WIND CALLING MY NAME!
JACKIE!

JAAAACKIE

JACKIE!
GET OUT OF THAT TUB, RIGHT NOW!

JACKIE, JACKIE!
All right, Mom!

YO HO